I Don't Care what You Wear as Long as It's Clean

Susie Rich

I Don't Care What You Wear as Long as It's Clean, Published November, 2015

Interior and Cover Illustrations: Randy Jennings
Interior Design & Layout: Howard Johnson, Howard Communigrafix, Inc.
Editorial and Proofreading: Eden Rivers Editorial Services; Karen Grennan
Author Photo: Nelson Nieves Photography

 SDP Publishing

Published by SDP Publishing, an imprint of SDP Publishing Solutions, LLC.

For more information about this book contact Lisa Akoury-Ross by email at lross@SDPPublishing.com.

SDP Publishing
Permissions Department
PO Box 26
East Bridgewater, MA 02333
or email your request to info@SDPPublishing.com.

ISBN-13 (print): 978-0-9964345-5-3

ISBN-13 (ebook): 978-0-9964345-6-0

Printed in the United States of America

"Good-bye honey," Tammy's dad said as he kissed Tammy on the forehead. "Have a wonderful day at the park," he added.

He also leaned over her baby brother, Tommy, as he sat in his high chair, and said, "See ya, Sport," as he tried giving Tommy a high five. Tommy giggled and raised both hands as Daddy smiled.

He kissed their mother on the way out the door and whispered, "Have a great day," as he went off to work.

"Mommy, Mommy," said Tammy, "can I wear my favorite blue jeans?"
Tammy was excited to get to the park.

"I don't care what you wear as long as it's clean," her mother answered as she placed plates in the sink. They had just finished a pleasant breakfast and now it was time to get ready for the park.

"Can I wear my blue shirt, the one with green seams?" asked Tammy.

"That's a good choice to wear as long as it's clean," answered her mother.

"What about my bright red hat with my sneakers that are green?" Tammy continued.

"Yes, baby, bright is nice; as long as they are clean."

9

Tammy put on her jeans with her blue shirt, bright red hat, white socks, and green sneakers. She ran to the mirror to see her outfit. Her mother was just sitting her little brother in his walker and said, "Watch Tommy, please, while I change; then we will go to the park."

"Sure, Mom," said Tammy as she stepped in front of the mirror. "Looking good," she thought, smiling—until she noticed something.

"What's that?" she said aloud, noticing a spot on her jeans. "A spot is not clean, get rid of the jeans," thought Tammy.

She went to her dresser and pulled out a pair of blue shorts that would match the blue shirt with the green seams. "Mom," she yelled. "Can I wear blue shorts to match my shirt with green seams?"

"I don't care what you wear," her mother answered, "as long as it's clean."

Tammy slipped on the shorts and went back to the mirror. As she passed, Tommy reached for her hand and laughed. "Yep, Tommy, we are going to the park today," she said to him.

She sat down on the bed in front of the mirror. "As soon as Mommy and I are dressed we are off."

"I'm pretty much ready," she said as she looked at herself in the
mirror again and smiled, but her smile didn't last long. "OH NO!"
she said, frowning.

"There's a spot on my shirt! Look, right on the shoulder," she
complained to Tommy. "How could I have missed that?" she
thought. "How could that spot not have been seen?" she wondered.

"I'm ready," said Mommy. "Are you wearing something clean?"

"Almost!" yelled Tammy. "I changed my mind about the shirt with the green seams."

"It doesn't matter what you wear," answered her mother, "just as long as it's clean."

Tammy helped Tommy as he scooted his walker in front of the mirror. This made it easier for her to get to the dresser and pick out her next outfit.

Tommy slumped into his walker watching quietly and sucking his thumb. "Good boy, Tommy. I'm sorry, I'm not trying to be mean. It's just that I have to wear something that's completely clean."

"Mom, I'm going with my green shirt with blue and red dots that match my sneakers that are green."

"OK, honey," said Mom. "That's fine, as long as it's clean."

Tammy put on the shirt and went to the mirror to see her new outfit choice. Tommy was square in front of the mirror so Tammy stood on the bed. "This way I can also see my shoes," she thought. A red hat, a green shirt with blue and red dots, a pair of blue shorts, white socks, and green sneakers to match. "Yes!" she said proudly and loudly … until she noticed something not clean.

A big spot on her sneakers now made them not completely green. "Another spot!" she thought. "What is that?" she said jumping down from the bed. Yet another spot she noticed, and this one was on her leg, above her left knee.

"What is this?" she whispered, "what could that be?" Just at that moment Mommy walked in with the stroller.

"Oh goodness," she said, picking up Tommy, who now was asleep.

"Mommy look, look! I have a dirty spot on me. First it was on my favorite blue jeans, then my blue shirt with the pretty green seams, then on my sneakers that are green, and now on me. I'm not even clean!"

"Oh, my love," said Mommy, "why are you making such a scene? The spot's on your mirror, which just needs to be cleaned."

Mommy strapped Tommy into his stroller. "It's not on you or your favorite blue jeans, it is not on your blue shirt with the green seams. It wasn't on your sneakers that are green, and it is not on you; you are completely clean."

"My love, the spot is on your mirror; you just need to remember to keep your mirror clean."

Tammy looked at her mother, smiled and said, "I guess I must remember to make my mirror gleam, as well as make sure I wear something clean."

"Yes," her mother agreed as they continued to get ready for the park.

"Mommy, when we get to the park can we play on the swings?"

"Yes," said her mother. "We can also play on the slides and do the climbing things."

"Can I play in the dirt and pretend to make cookies and cream?" asked Tammy.

"Sure, if you want to, and maybe after we will get real ice cream," her mother answered.

25

"Mommy," Tammy asked, "you know that I will be dirty after we do all of these things, so why did it really matter that I wear something clean?"

"We should always try and look our best when we go out and can be seen, and it always makes me happy when my children wear something clean," Mommy said.

Tammy's mother looked down at her and smiled. They both giggled as the three of them headed home after enjoying their day at the park.

ABOUT THE AUTHOR

Susie Rich was raised in Cincinnati, Ohio, and has spent her career working in the social work/homelessness prevention field. Several years ago, she began to pursue her passion for writing; she has published "Beauties, The Eye of the Beholder," in an Ohio magazine, and two children's books: *How My Daddy Taught Me to Dance* and *Too Much Hopscotch*. She also has written a number of short stories and is currently working on a novel. She resides near Boston, Massachusetts, with her husband, Douglas.

I Don't Care What You Wear as Long as It's Clean
Susie Rich

Children's book

Also by Susie Rich

How My Daddy Taught Me to Dance

Too Much Hopscotch

Children's books

Author Website: www.SusiesStories.com

Also available in ebook format
TO PURCHASE:
Amazon.com
BarnesAndNoble.com
SDPPublishing.com

 SDP Publishing

www.SDPPublishing.com

Contact us at: info@SDPPublishing.com

CPSIA information can be obtained
at www.ICGtesting.com
Printed in the USA
LVHW071650130720
660549LV00015B/2345